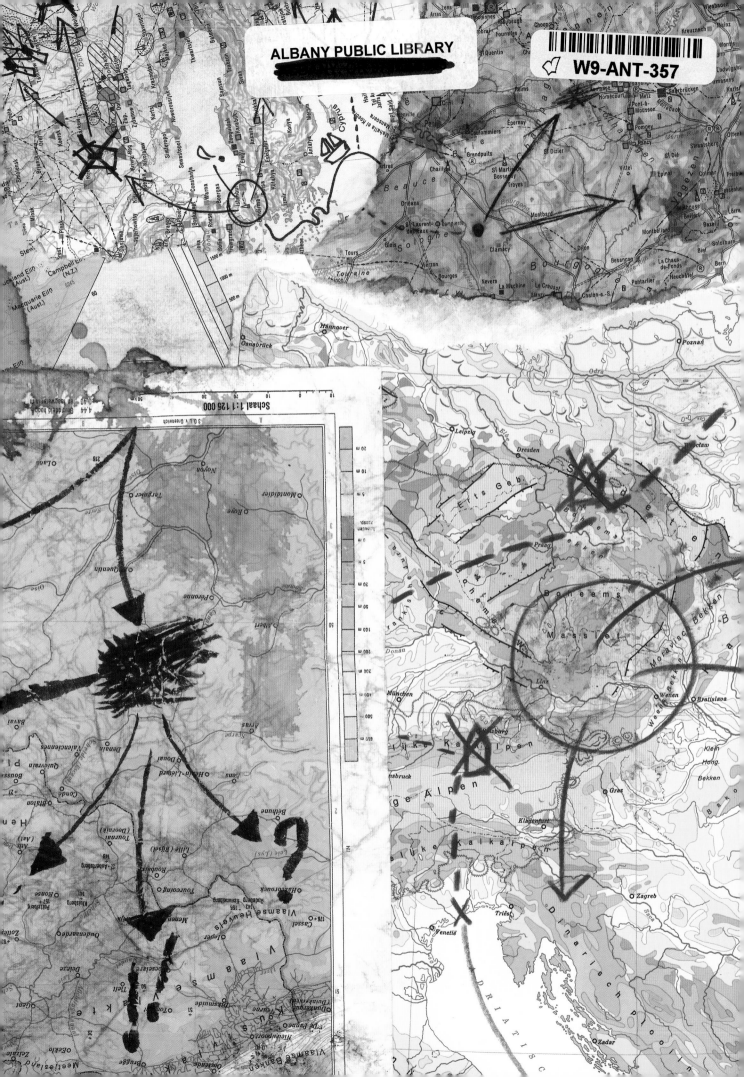

Text © 2020 Flyaway Books
Illustrations © 2019 Yoeri Slegers

Original title: *Krokodil op weg naar beter* © 2019 by Uitgeverij De Eenhoorn, Vlasstraat 17, B-8710 Wielsbeke (Belgium)

First English edition
Published by Flyaway Books
Louisville, Kentucky

20 21 22 23 24 25 26 27 28 29–10 9 8 7 6 5 4 3 2 1

Book design by Allison Taylor
Text set in Adderville ITC Std

Library of Congress Cataloging-in-Publication Data

Names: Slegers, Yoeri, author, illustrator.
Title: Crocodile's crossing : a search for home / Yoeri Slegers.
Other titles: Krokodil op weg naar beter. English
Description: First English edition. | Louisville, Kentucky : Flyaway Books,
  [2020] | Originally published in Dutch in Wielsbeke, Belgium by
  Uitgeverij De Eenhoorn in 2019 under title: Krokodil op weg naar beter.
  | Audience: Ages 3-7. | Audience: Grades K-1. | Summary: Crocodile is
  tired, scared, and hopeful as he searches for a new home.
Identifiers: LCCN 2019040216 | ISBN 9781947888210 (hardback)
Subjects: CYAC: Emigration and immigration--Fiction. | Prejudices--Fiction.
  | Crocodiles--Fiction.
Classification: LCC PZ7.1.S5885 Cr 2020 | DDC [E]--dc23
LC record available at https://lccn.loc.gov/2019040216

PRINTED IN CHINA

Most Flyaway Books are available at special quantity discounts when purchased in bulk by corporations, organizations, and special-interest groups.
For more information, please e-mail SpecialSales@flyawaybooks.com.

YOERI SLEGERS

CROCODILE'S CROSSING

A Search for Home

flyaway books

Crocodile was on his way.
He was tired. Scared. Hopeful.
*Everything will be better
where I'm going!* he thought.
But where is that?

Crocodile once had a home that he loved.
He had a cozy bed and good food.
He had friends. He had a family.
He was safe and happy.

But then the trouble started.
Home wasn't safe anymore.
There wasn't enough food.
Everything grew worse and worse.

Finally, Crocodile knew he had to find a better place.
He packed his red backpack. He gave his home one last look.
He hugged his family and hoped he would see them again.
Then he went on his way.

Crocodile's journey was long and hard.
He went to one place and then another.

Everywhere, houses and food and clothes and words
were so different from what he knew.
Crocodile couldn't find a place that felt like home.
He couldn't find anyone to welcome him.

"You're so big! So green!" everyone cried.
"Those enormous teeth look so dangerous.
Nobody wants a crocodile here.

Go away!"

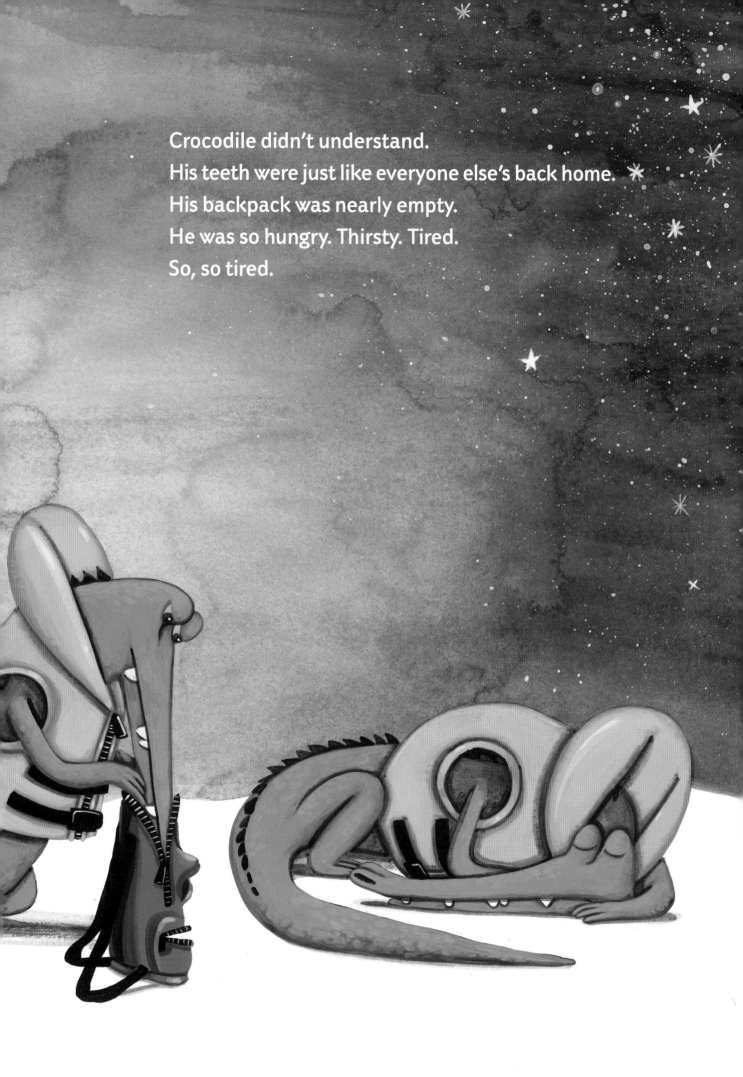

Crocodile didn't understand.
His teeth were just like everyone else's back home.
His backpack was nearly empty.
He was so hungry. Thirsty. Tired.
So, so tired.

Every night, he dreamed of home.
Then one morning . . .

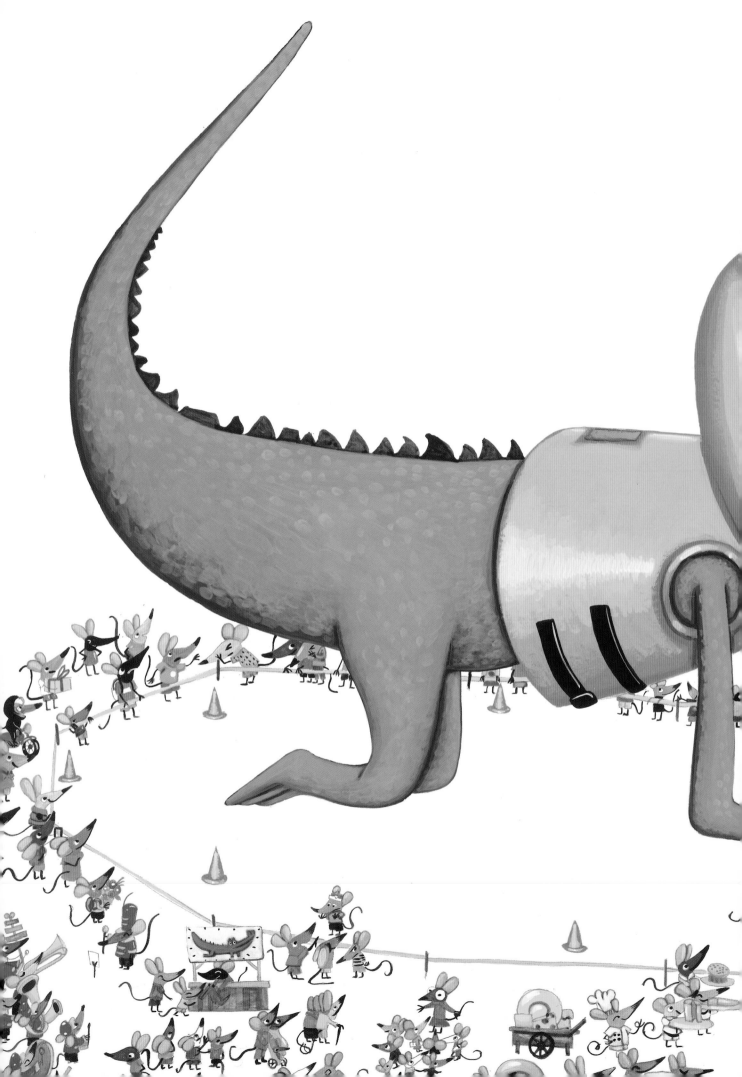

"Good morning," said a small voice. "Do you want some tea?"
Who could that be? Crocodile opened his eyes.
What are all these mice up to? But tea did sound good.
"Thank you," he said.
"Are you hungry? We have some cheese," said the mouse.
"I've never heard of cheese," said Crocodile, "but I'll try it."

As time went by, Crocodile tasted more new things.
He was still big. Still green. His teeth were still enormous.
But the mice didn't mind. After a while, neither did Crocodile.
He watched and listened. He learned new skills.
One day, he even helped with a rescue!

"Thanks, Crocodile!" the mice cheered.
"Friends take care of one another," Crocodile said.

Crocodile came to like this place. It began to feel more like home.
He ate good food with his new friends.
He had a house with a warm bed. He was safe.
But something was still missing.
So he worked, waited, and hoped, until . . .

at last, one day,
the missing piece arrived.